GREAT JOB, MOM!

Holman Wang

tundra

Tundra Books, an imprint of Penguin Random House Canada Young Readers,
a Penguin Random House Company

Library and Archives Canada Cataloguing in Publication

Wang, Holman, author, illustrator
     Great job, Mom! / Holman Wang.

Issued in print and electronic formats.
ISBN 978-0-7352-6408-3 (hardcover).—ISBN 978-0-7352-6409-0 (ebook)

     I. Title.

PS8645.A5318G76 2019   jC813'.6   C2018-900666-8
                                                C2018-900667-6

Published simultaneously in the United States of America by Tundra Books of Northern New York,
an imprint of Penguin Random House Canada Young Readers, a Penguin Random House Company

Library of Congress Control Number: 2018935605

Edited by Samantha Swenson
Designed by Kelly Hill and John Martz

The artwork in this book was created through needle felting (in wool),
scale-model set making and photography.
The text was set in Avenir LT Pro.
Drawings on refrigerator by Celia Wang and Felix Wang
Endpaper texture by Pannonia/Getty Images

Printed and bound in China

www.penguinrandomhouse.ca

1 2 3 4 5   23 22 21 20 19

For Amy

My mom works as a **carpenter**.
She builds things big and strong.

At night, though, she's a **general**
who'll march the troops along.

She's also part-time **curator**
with passion for the arts.

And frequent **archaeologist**

in search of buried parts.

She's very much a **scientist** —

there's data year by year.

And **Secret Service agent**, too,

who follows very near.

On most days she's a **journalist** on top of breaking news.

But sometimes she's a **zookeeper**
who handles beastly crews.

She serves as **doctor** now and then
when patients must be nursed.

At times she has an **actor**'s flair —

without a line rehearsed!

And **DJ** is the late-night gig
she never tires of.

Mom does one job for her career,
the others out of love.

BEHIND THE SCENES
with Holman Wang

I think of my illustration process as something akin to moviemaking. First, I cast the characters. In my case, I create 1:6 scale figures in wool through needle felting — a painstaking process of sculpting wool by repeatedly stabbing it with a specialized barbed needle.

Next, I scout locations for outdoor photography, build scale-model sets for indoor shoots and acquire or make all the pint-sized props I need for particular scenes. Then I get behind the camera! After a lot of trial and error, I usually manage to capture an image that's worthy of the final step: a little digital editing in post-production.

Sometimes, my photographs borrow a technique which was common in B movies of the 1950s and 1960s: forced perspective. This is an optical illusion where an object may appear smaller or larger, or nearer or farther away, than it actually is.

By using a short focal length and placing the scale-model sets and wool figures close to the camera, I was able to seamlessly integrate the foreground miniatures in the same photograph with real-life outdoor backdrops and even rooms in my own house. It's not quite Hollywood, but hopefully you'll find a little magic just the same.

Holman Wang is a lawyer who also finds time to make children's books. He and his brother, Jack, are the twin powers behind the board book series Cozy Classics and Star Wars Epic Yarns, which abridge literary and cinematic classics into just twelve words and twelve needle-felted images.

In 2015, Holman and Jack created a Google Doodle celebrating Laura Ingalls Wilder. Their unique artwork has been exhibited around the world, including at The Original Art exhibition in New York (Society of Illustrators), the Bologna Children's Book Fair and the National Museum of Play.

Holman lives with his wife and kids in Vancouver, Canada.

Visit his website at **www.holmanwang.com**